Paca
and His Pals Visit St. Simons Island

y: Jeffrey W. Young I & Jeffrey W. Young III (Trey) • Illustrations By: Joe McCormick

Are we there yet?
Are we there yet?
Are we there yet?
Almost.....Just one more bridge.

I see the sign!!
We're here.....
Yipee! Yipee! Yipee!

Hooray, Whoo-Hoo, yay.....
We made it!
Look there's Nina on the porch
Run, hurry!

Papa, Papa, We're here, we're here!
When can we go to the Beach?
Paca, Trey, get the beach toys and
load the beachcart and we will go.

Let's Go!
Whoopee I can't wait....Will the tide
be up? I hope we find some sand dollars.
Hey, did anybody bring any potato chips?

Papa, Relax, Nina Look.....
we are building a
sandcastle!

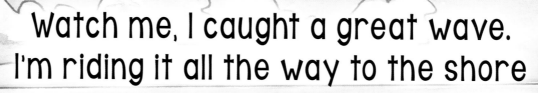

Watch me, I caught a great wave.
I'm riding it all the way to the shore

Look!!! Brandt. I found a sand dollar!!

Here's Barbara Jean's.
Can we eat here? They have the best
crabcakes! I like their chicken fried chicken.
Hey, what about that yummy
Pumpkin bread?

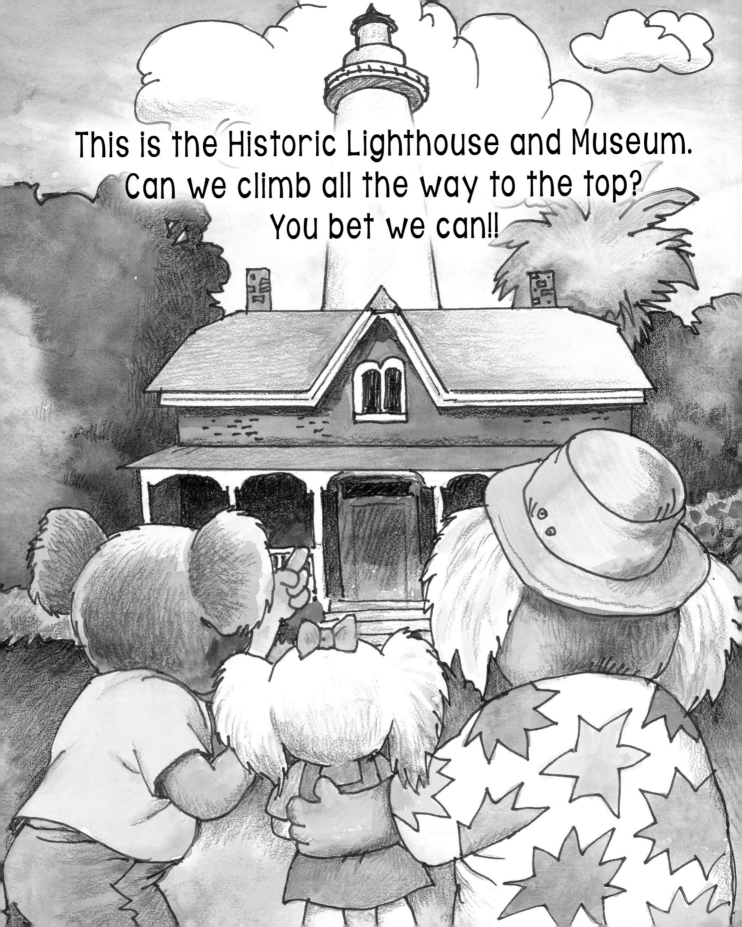

Wow!
You can see everything from up here!
Everyone looks so small!
Wave at Nina, she's down there by the palm tree.

This is the old Coast Guard Station.
It's got a lot of neat Navy and Coast Guard stuff in it.
Hurry, I can't wait to see it all!

Maritime Cen
Historic Coast Guard

The Coast Guard helps boats and seamen when they get in trouble on the water. Preston it says, "back during World War II a German Submarine sunk two ships right here in the channel off of St. Simons Island."

Trying to find all of the Tree Spirits is fun!
We have found five. Count them... one, two,
three, four..........

The shrimp boats drop their nets just off shore.
Look at these tasty fresh caught shrimp.
Can we have some for supper?

Here is St. Simons Bait & Tackle Shop.
Before we go fishing we have to stop and
get some bait, don't forget the hooks and sinkers.
Can we talk to Byrd before we leave?
Sure, everyone loves Byrd!

Let's walk down to the pier and go fishing.
People come from all over to fish and catch blue crabs.

Climbing to the top of
the whale's head can be hard.
Can you help me get to the top?

Nina's favorite place, She loves to sit in the rockers on the porch and watch us play.

Fort Frederica founded in 1733...
This was the first English Settlement
on the island.

Stopping by to see...
Historic Christ Church Frederica.

Off to adventures. Riding
our bikes under the
Majestic Live Oaks.

Exploring Driftwood Beach!
This is amazing!!

found a Horseshoe
Crab!
I can see a shrimp
boat from here.

Enjoying this beautiful sunset!
Once you walked the sandy beaches
of St. Simons Island.....
The sand in your shoes they say, is
sure to bring you back!

Good-bye.....Good-bye.....
Come back and see us!
We've had such a wonderful time.

Good-bye St. Simons Island.....
this has been the best trip, EVER!!